SuperHero ABC

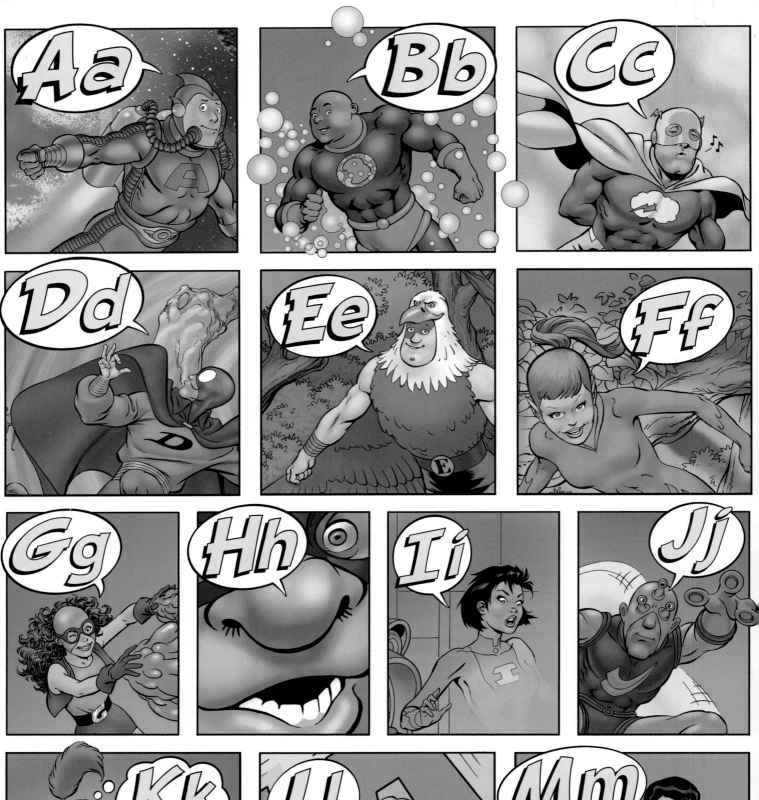

THIS BOOK IS DEDICATED TO MY WONDERFUL WIFE, LUCY, WHOSE BRILLIANT IDEA IT WAS, AND WHO'S BEEN WAITING, SOMEWHAT PATIENTLY, FOR OVER TWENTY YEARS FOR ME TO DO A CHILDREN'S BOOK! I HOPE THIS IS JUST THE FIRST OF MANY. I'D ALSO LIKE TO THANK MY WHOLE FAMILY FOR THEIR CONSTANT LOVING SUPPORT AND HELP, AND ALSO THE EMMAUS PUBLIC LIBRARY STAFF FOR THEIR ENTHUSIASTIC ENCOURAGEMENT. SPECIAL THANKS TO LISA DUGAN FOR HER INVALUABLE ASSISTANCE CONNECTING ME WITH HARPERCOLLINS, AND TO MARGARET, MY SUPEREDITOR.

ISBN-13: 978-545-03604-7
ISBN-10: 0-545-03604-6

12 11 10 9 8 7 6 5 4 3 2 1   7 8 9 10 11 12/0

Printed in the U.S.A.   08

First Scholastic printing, September 2007
Typography by Meredith Pratt

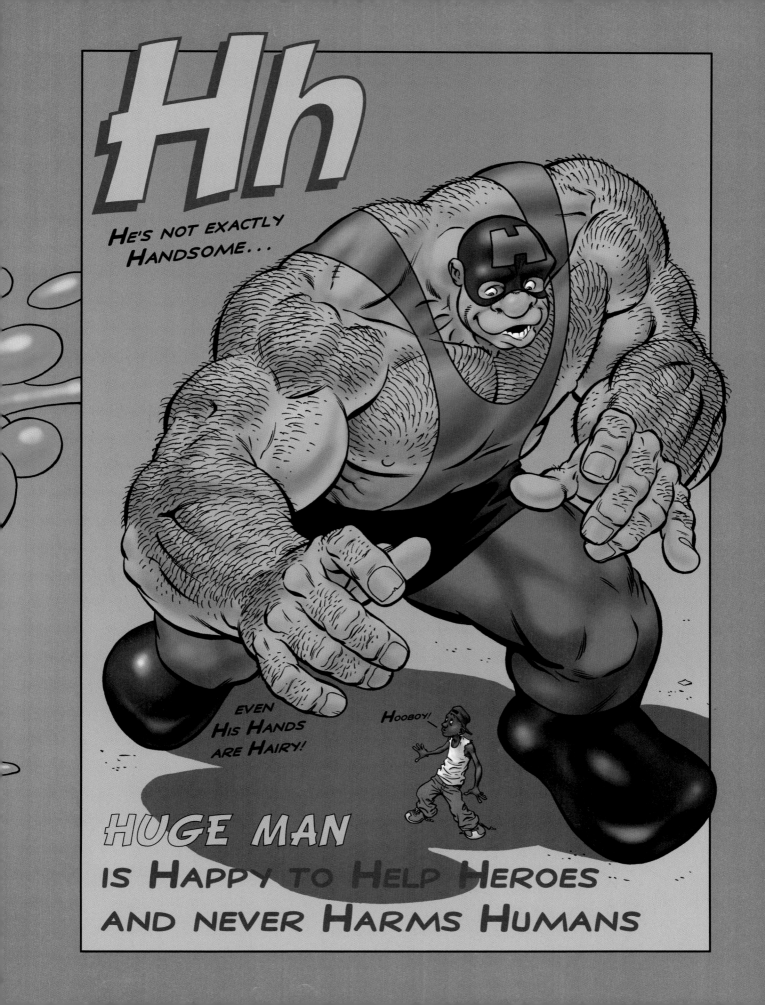

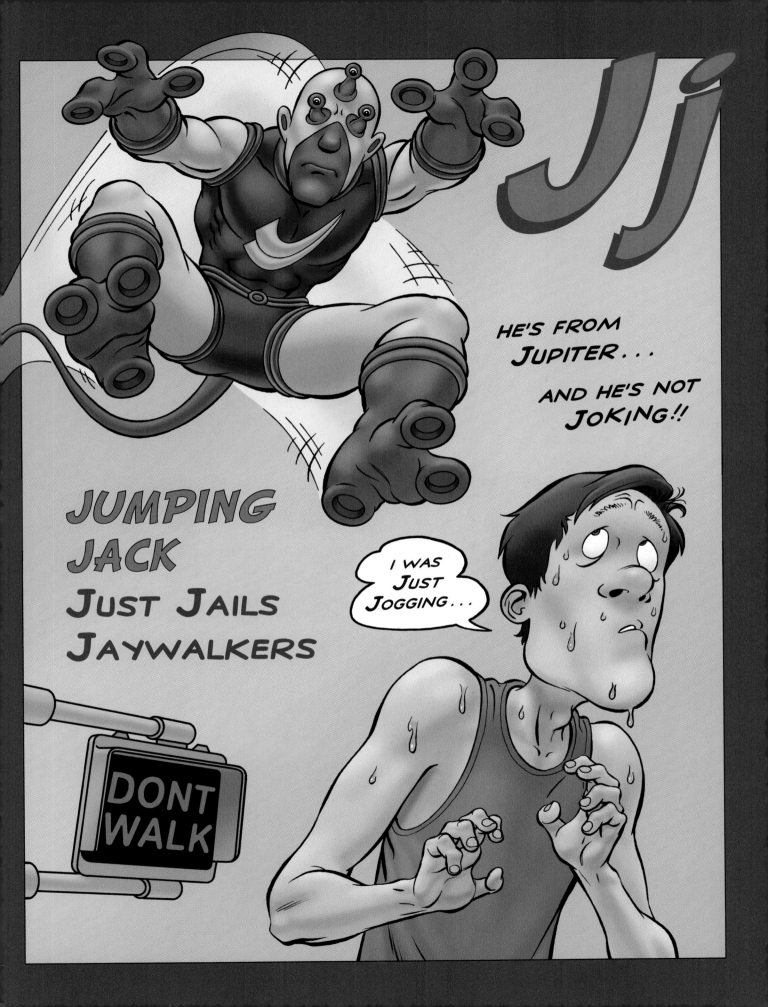

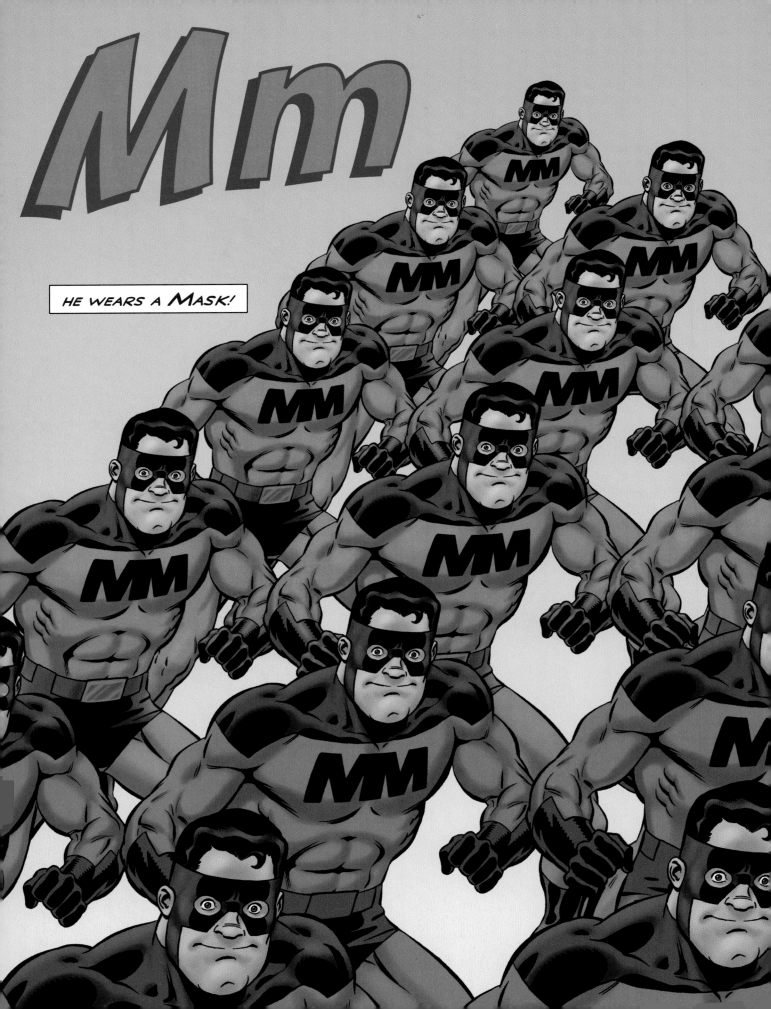

Rr

RAIN-MAN
RAINS ON
RANDOM ROBBERS

HIS COSTUME IS RED RUBBER! REALLY!

RATS!

HE'S A RIOT!

BUT RATHER RUDE...

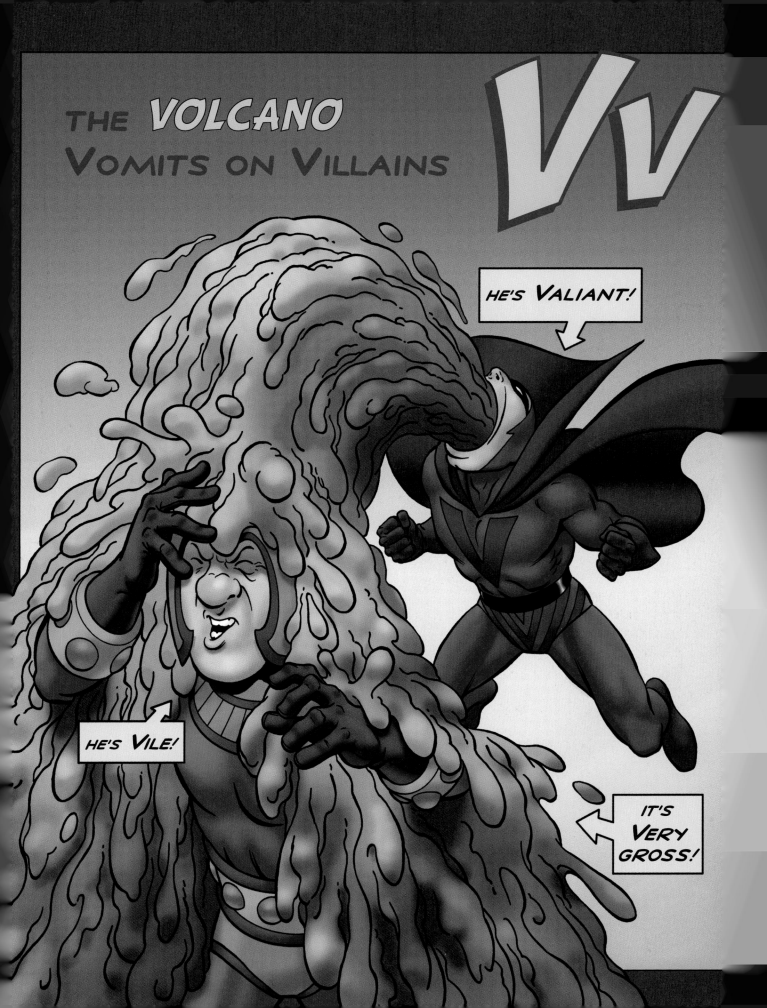

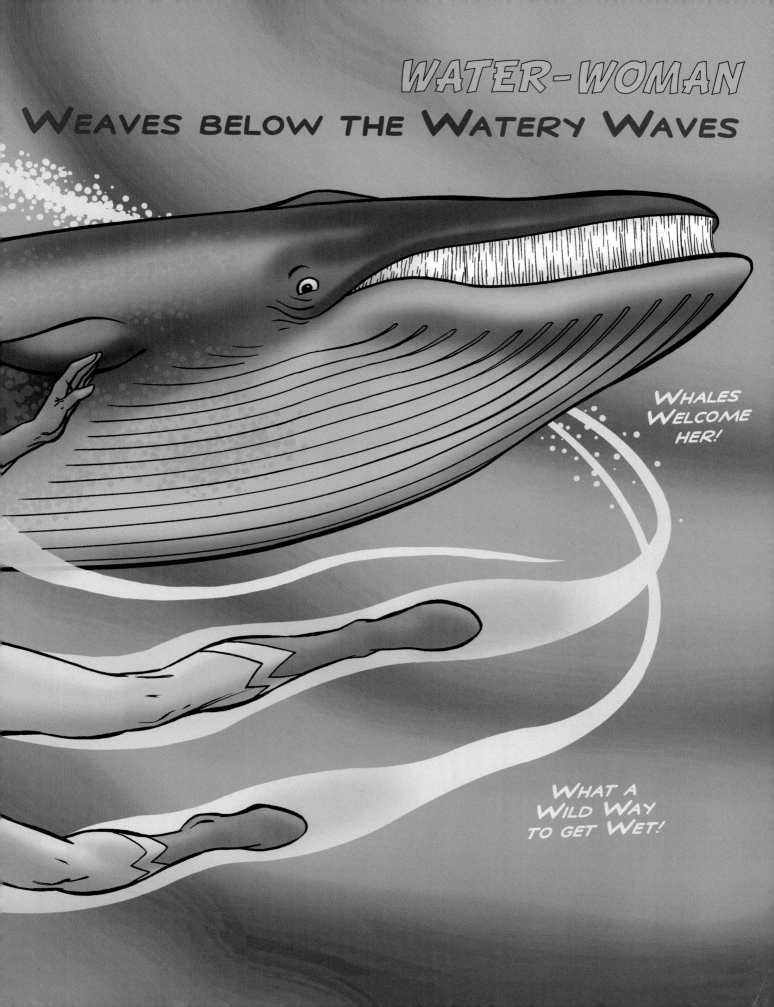

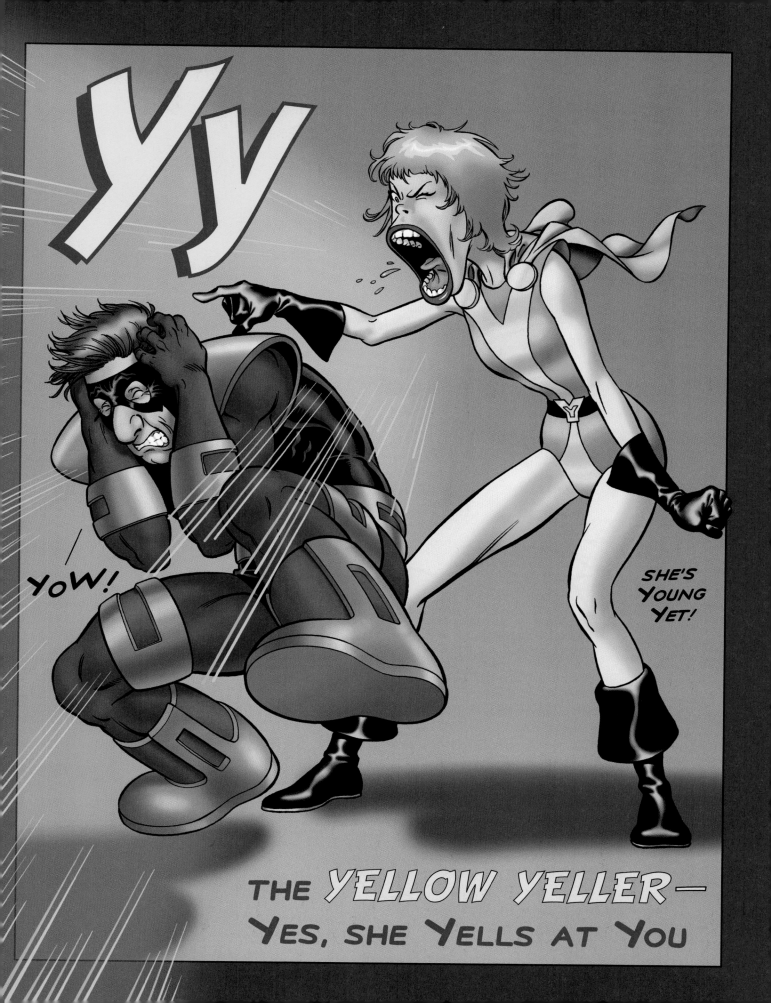

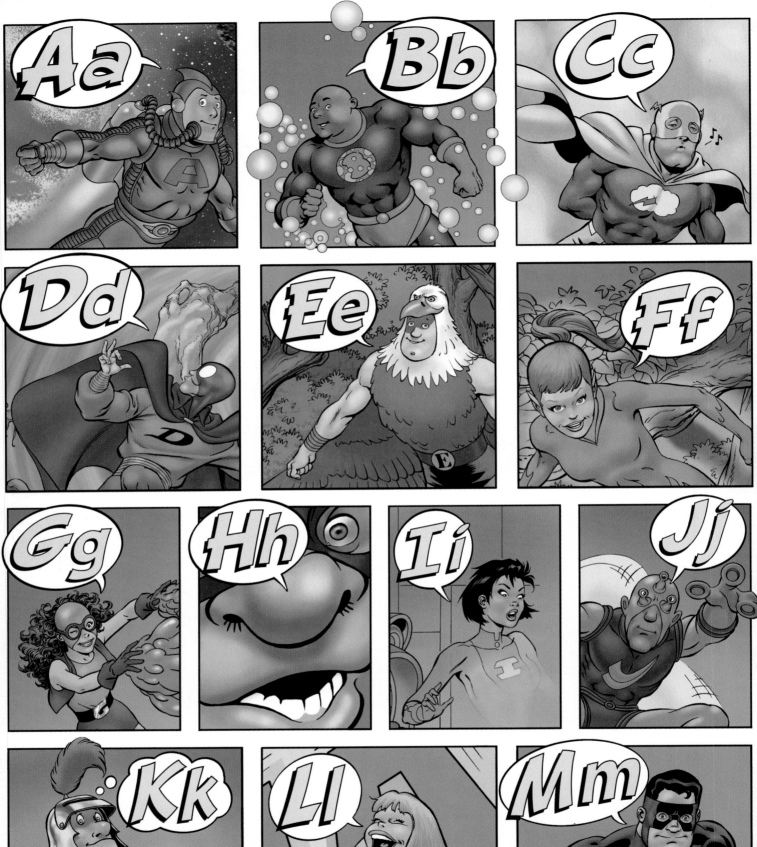